This book belongs to

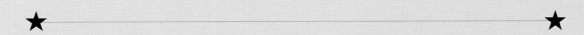

This edition published by Parragon in 2007

Parragon
Queen Street House
4 Queen Street
Bath BA1 1HE, UK

ISBN 978-1-4054-1021-2

Printed in China

Please retain this information for future reference

THE PRINCESS and the MAGIC LOCKET

Written by Nick Ellsworth ★ Illustrated by Veronica Vasylenko

PaRragon

Bath · New York · Singapore · Hong Kong · Cologne · Delhi · Melbourne

It was Princess Crystal's birthday. Her father, the King, had invited everyone to a party at the palace. The King gave Princess Crystal a very special present – a beautiful locket. "This is a magical locket," the King told Princess Crystal. "But, it will only work if you say the magic rhyme:

"Magical locket,
please listen well:
Help my friend
with a kindly spell."

No one noticed the wicked witch, peeping through the window. When she saw the magic locket, the witch wanted it for herself.

The next day, Princess Crystal
went riding on her favourite horse.
She didn't see the witch hiding
behind a tree.
As Princess Crystal trotted by,
the wicked witch cast her evil spell:

"Frogs and toads,
and all things black,
Throw the princess
on her back!"

Princess Crystal's horse reared up, and threw her to the ground.
As quick as a flash, the wicked witch took the locket from around
Princess Crystal's neck.

"Now, the locket's mine!" she cackled, and hurried away.

When Princess Crystal opened her eyes, she
saw a young prince.

"Are you hurt, your Highness?" asked the prince.

"I don't think so," said Princess Crystal sitting up.
She felt a bit dizzy from her fall.

"Who are you?" she asked.

"Prince Robert," replied the prince with
a smile. "I saw you fall from your horse."

When she felt better, Prince Robert gently
helped her back onto her horse,
and led them to the palace gates.

"I shall not forget your kindness," said
Princess Crystal. The prince bowed and,
turning to wave goodbye, walked back
towards the forest.

Meanwhile, the wicked witch
was in her tower trying to make the
locket's magic work.

"Slimy snails,
and things that lurk,
Make this magical
locket work!"

She stood back, hoping to see some
magic... but nothing happened.

"Fur of cat,
and eye of bee.
Open the locket's
secret to me!"

Again, nothing happened.

"Boil and bubble,
and all things bad,
Make it work,
or I'll go MAD!"

Still, nothing happened.
The witch screamed and yelled, and
pulled at her hair and stamped her feet.
All of a sudden, she had an idea.

Meanwhile, Princess Crystal realised that she
had lost her magical locket. She decided to ride
back to the forest to thank Prince Robert
for helping her, and to ask him
if he had found the locket.
But the witch was waiting for
her up a tree. As soon as
Princess Crystal rode by,
the witch threw a net over her,
bundled the frightened princess over
her shoulder and carried her away.
"I've caught you!" cackled the witch.
Soon they arrived at the witch's tower.
A fierce dragon guarded it.
"Don't try to escape, my pretty one,"
said the witch, "or Horace the dragon
will eat you up!"

At the top of the tower, the witch freed her.
"Do you remember this?" she asked, holding up the magical locket.
"My locket!" gasped Princess Crystal.
"Yes," hissed the witch. "I stole it from you,
and now I want the magic rhyme to go with it."

"I won't give it to you," said Princess Crystal bravely.

"Then you can stay here until you do!" shouted the witch.

"Here's your precious locket," she said, throwing it at Princess Crystal. "It won't do you any good in here!"

She stormed out of the room, locking the door behind her.

Princess Crystal felt so alone. She leaned out of the window and began to cry. Her tears fell onto Horace the dragon below.

"You're making me all wet," he said grumpily, flying up to the window. "I'm not crying, even though my wing's broken, and really hurts."

"Oh, you poor thing," said Princess Crystal feeling sorry for the dragon. "Maybe I can help you." She closed her eyes, held the locket and said the magic rhyme:

"Magical locket,
please listen well:
Help my friend
with a kindly spell."

Princess Crystal opened her eyes, and saw that Horace's wing had completely healed. "Oh, thank you," he said happily. "My wing is healed, and I don't feel grumpy any more. But what can I do to return your kindness?"

"Fly to the forest as quick as you can and find help,"
she said. Horace promised he'd go quickly,
and beating his wings he rose into the air.

Soon, Horace was flying high over the forest.

Horace found Prince Robert. When he heard that Princess Crystal had been captured by the witch, he jumped onto Horace's back and flew to the rescue.

As they approached the tower, Prince Robert could see Princess Crystal waving from the tower. Horace flew right up to the window. "Thank goodness Horace found you," cried Princess Crystal, as Prince Robert climbed in through the window. But before they could escape, the door suddenly opened.

There stood the wicked witch.
"How nice of you to join us,
young man," cackled the witch.
"And, how handsome you are!

"But I think you'd look much
better... as a FROG!"
She began to cast an evil spell.

"Oh, no," thought Princess Crystal. "I'd better do something quickly."
She closed her eyes, held the locket and whispered the magic rhyme:

"Magical locket,
please listen well:
Help my friend
with a kindly spell."

When Princess Crystal
opened her eyes,
the locket's magic
had worked.

The witch's spell had backfired, and turned her
into a frog instead!
"Frogspawn and slime!" croaked the frog,
then it hopped out of the window, and was never
seen again.

"Thank you, your Highness," said Prince Robert,
"for saving me from becoming a frog!"
"But you helped me when I fell off my horse, and you
came to rescue me from the witch," said Princess Crystal,
smiling at him. And soon they were flying home.

The King was delighted to
see his daughter returned
safely. As a reward, the King
gave Horace a gleaming
new tower.
Princess Crystal and Prince
Robert became great friends.

"I'll take care of my precious
magical locket for ever and ever,"
Princess Crystal promised.